JUSTICE LEAGUE UNLIMITED

DEFENDERS OF THE PLANET

Written by Heather Au
Designed by Chris Fowler

BENDON®
Publishing International, Inc.

Ashland, OH 44805
www.bendonpub.com

Far beyond earth in outer space, the Justice League keeps careful watch over the planet below. The team's hovering headquarters, The Watchtower, allows these defenders of Earth to patrol the planet from afar.

Should an emergency arise, the team uses their spacecraft, the Javelin-7, to transport them back to Earth.

When these heroes unite, evildoers beware!

As a baby, Kal-El was rocketed to Earth by his parents in an attempt to save their son from the doomed Planet Krypton. The baby was found and quickly made his new home with the Kent family. The family named the baby Clark and raised him as their own.

Clark was a respectable young man. As he grew, Clark began to realize that he had powers and abilities unlike any human.

He moved to Metropolis, becoming a news reporter for the Daily Planet and...the world's greatest super hero—Superman!

When evil strikes, Superman is equipped to fight and ready to defend. With his super-strength and amazing speed, he can stop any villain that crosses his path.

BATMAN™

Batman is the World's Greatest Detective--a crime fighter with many skills and talents. He spends his days playing the role of billionaire Bruce Wayne. But at night, he puts on the mask and cape of Batman, protector of Gotham City!

Batman works alone and likes to stay in the shadows, but when the Justice League calls, the Dark Knight answers!

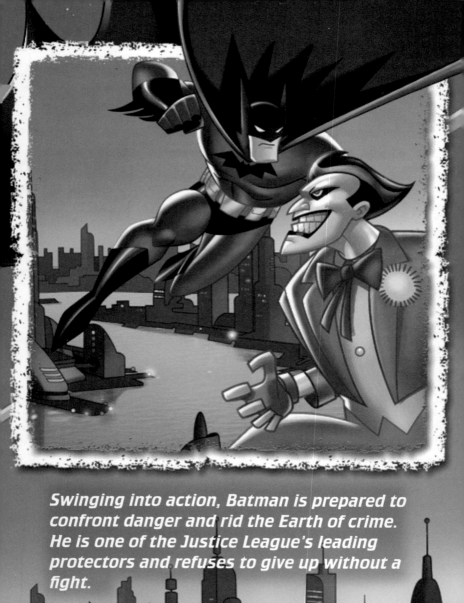

Swinging into action, Batman is prepared to confront danger and rid the Earth of crime. He is one of the Justice League's leading protectors and refuses to give up without a fight.

As Princess of the Amazons, Diana was granted mighty powers. With her amazing speed and strength, she protects Earth as Wonder Woman!

Wonder Woman's powers and natural skill make her a threat in any battle. Her magical silver bracelets can be used for defense, while her Golden Lasso demands honesty from those in its grasp.

Young Wally West was visiting a laboratory when a bolt of lightning crashed through the window and shattered a nearby rack of chemicals. The chemicals spilled on Wally, giving him the power of super-speed and transforming him into the Flash—the Fastest Man Alive!

Defending the Earth with his teammates, the Flash is the speediest member of the Justice League!

THE FLASH

John Stewart is a member of the Green Lantern Corps, an intergalactic police force founded by the Guardians of Oa.

Green Lantern uses his power ring to create unbreakable force fields and powerful energy beams. The ring's aura protects him from the elements of outer space, where he has been on active duty for years.

Joining the Justice League, the Green Lantern has returned home to protect the planet Earth.

J'onn J'onzz, the Martian Manhunter, is the last survivor of an ancient Martian race. The Martian Manhunter can read minds and use his shape-shifting power to turn himself into anyone—or anything—he chooses!

J'onn came to Earth to warn us of an invasion by the evil race that wiped out his own people on Mars. He helped form a group of heroes who could fight off the invaders. This group was the Justice League!

HAWKGIRL

Shayera Hol was a police detective on her home planet of Thanagar. While chasing criminals, she was hit by a weapon that transported her halfway across the galaxy!

Quickly coming to admire the people of Earth, Shayera became fascinated by ancient Egyptian tales of hawk-like beings.

Now, as Hawkgirl, she uses her mace and Thanagarian powers to protect her adopted home.

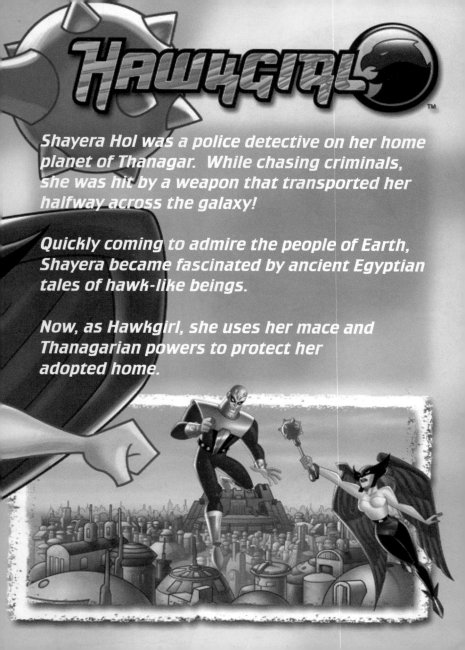

Strength. Power. Courage.

When these bold and brave heroes unite, evildoers beware! In their never-ending mission to protect Earth, the Justice League is ready for action!